ADVENTURES IN
WILLŌGA

The Fifth Power

Conall O'Dowd

ISBN: 978-1537151793

Published by NINTAI PUBLICATIONS
Printed by CREATESPACE

Acknowledgements

I would like to thank the following people, who helped make this book possible:

Claire Loughran, who created the cover picture.

Ruth Callinan and Djinn von Noorden for reviewing and editing.

My friends, for allowing me to use their names as characters.

My Dad, for his encouragement.

Contents

Chapter 1
THE STORY BEGINS   I

Chapter 2
THE EYES   8

Chapter 3
THE SPY   14

Chapter 4
HELP AT LAST   16

Chapter 5
THE AMBUSH   19

Chapter 6
ZTARAS   23

Chapter 7
THE MOUNTAIN   29

Chapter 8
THE DRABONZ 35

Chapter 9
THE PLAN 39

Chapter 10
RAGER 43

Chapter 11
THE FIGHT! 46

Chapter 12
AT LAST! 51

Chapter 13
THE QUEEN 62

ADVENTURES IN WILLŌGA

The Fifth Power

THE STORY BEGINS

Daniel, Charlie, Katie and Alice are best friends. They all live on the same street, and they are all in the same class in school. They have known each other since before they started school and always go to each others' houses. They quite often meet up after school and the parents of the four say they could nearly be brothers and sisters. Although they are great friends and go everywhere together, they have some different interests.

Charlie has pale blue eyes and raven black hair. He is tall and very strong. He loves swimming, and goes every weekend with his dad and the others to the local swimming pool. He is very good at it and his dad calls him his 'little fish'.

Alice has freckles, brown eyes and blondish-brown hair. She is of average height for her age, and is almost always cheerful. She loves gardening and planting things. One time her class was helping with the school garden, and everything that Alice planted grew better and taller than anything else. She says she just loves the feel of her hands in the soil.

Katie has long, dark brown hair. She is slightly taller than Alice. Katie is interested in weather and especially loves to watch programmes about tornadoes and hurricanes. This started because she once went to America and actually saw a small tornado, which they called a 'twister'. She was fascinated.

Daniel has dark brown skin and black hair. He is the youngest of the four and is a bit smaller than Alice. Daniel wants be a fireman when he grows up. He has a great fireman's outfit, which he wears every Halloween. He also has lots of remote-controlled fire trucks and other toys. And, of course, he loved *Fireman Sam* when he was younger.

The four friends were walking to school one morning. They lived close to the school, so they were often the first people in the class. They opened the door to their classroom and suddenly a portal the size of a doorway appeared in front of them. It looked like it was a made out of multicoloured clouds swirling around each other. It was all blues, purples, oranges and reds. Before they could react, it sucked them in.

They found themselves in a different, bizarre, new world. There were large, tree-covered rocks suspended in the purple sky, which looked like floating islands. They were held up by some unexplainable force. In the distance, there were two suns setting: one yellow sun and a larger red sun. There were strange creatures surrounding them. They had bull-like faces, some with a ring going through their noses, others with their noses simply pierced. Their ears were cat-like and they wore shorts and had their muscular torsos exposed. Their arms were big and strong and on their hands was a device, which looked like a leather glove with five long, nasty-looking metal blades protruding out of the top.

The four were scared, but then a man, who looked to be in his thirties and was dressed in a blue robe, which blew around behind him, appeared in front of them.

"Welcome," he said. "My name is Rizley. Thank you for coming."

"What do you mean? Where are we?" blurted out Daniel.

"You are in Willōga," replied the man. "We sent for you to help us."

"Help you?" asked Alice, looking nervously over her shoulder at the monsters that were getting closer. "How can we help you?"

"We need your talents," explained Rizley. "These monsters are destroying our planet. They are controlled by Rager, who is an evil warlord, and he is searching for special powers to defeat whoever stands in the way between him, and, as clichéd as it sounds, world domination. His aim? To be unstoppable. He wants your powers and only you and your powers can stop him. In your world, the things that you are interested in have become real powers in our world. You four control the elements of air, earth, fire and water between you. We need you to use these powers to fight the monsters and defeat Rager."

The four friends didn't believe Rizley, but soon they found that he was right; they did have strange new powers. As the monsters started to advance towards them, they became louder and more menacing. The four friends, encouraged by Rizley, sprang into action.

Daniel found that he was able to create and control fire. As he became scared and angry at the same time, his hands started to heat up and felt himself connect with the heat. He reacted on instinct. He shouted "Fire!" and stretched out his arms, and fire shot from them towards the monsters, forcing them back and scorching them.

Charlie thought about the amount of water there must be around them and he realised then that he could actually feel it. He found that he could connect with it and call it to join together. He shouted "Water!" and water rose up from the ground and shot in jets at the monsters, knocking them over.

Katie realised she could sense everyone's and everything's movements around her and could feel the air and the wind. She shouted "Air!" and a strong wind pushed the monsters even further back.

Finally, Alice shouted "Earth!" and the ground rose up under the monsters' feet, and then dropped suddenly, and gravity did the rest. The monsters had had enough – they ran away and didn't look back.

"What were those creatures?" Katie asked.

"They were zhouls, the evil and powerful monsters that Rager bred specifically for his evil army," said Rizley.

Rizley led the four friends to his cottage. It was small and white, and blue ivy grew here and there on the outside walls. It had orange smoke coming out of the chimney and gave the kids a nice warm feeling inside. Rizley invited them inside, and they sat down, excited and scared by what had just happened. He gave them a strange drink.

"This will help you keep your strength," he said. Then he told them where they would have to go to find Rager. "The Tallest Mountain is where Rager performs most of his work, and it has become a sort of HQ for them."

"Where do we find it?" Daniel asked.

Rizley looked serious. "It is a long way from here and it is a difficult journey," he told them. "However, I have no doubt that it will pay off."

After they rested he gave them some directions and a backpack with lots of food, a map, two types of compass and other things that could help them on their journey. Then he told them it was time to leave.

"I cannot go with you, because I have to help the people here."

And so the kids set off alone into this strange new world, armed only with their new-found powers.

Chapter 2

THE EYES

The four friends set off. Before long, they came to the remains of a village. Almost all of the buildings were destroyed and those that were still there were in ruins. Even so, they spotted a boy, around their age, watching them. Cautiously, they went over and introduced themselves. His name was Ethan and he told the kids that the village had been pillaged on Rager's order, but that all the inhabitants were safe because they were hiding in their basements, for fear of being attacked again by the zhouls. The friends told him that they were going to the Tallest Mountain to defeat Rager and his army.

"There's a river you need to cross to get out of here, but the zhouls destroyed the bridge," Ethan told them. "You'll have to go follow the bank south till you get to the next bridge. It'll be nightfall by then, so …"

"Don't worry," said Charlie. "We can get across."

Ethan noticed the confidence in Charlie's voice and was curious so he showed them to the river. It was very wide and no doubt very deep. The banks were cut and he could feel the water's strong current.

"I won't be able to stop all this water because I'm still getting used to my powers, but I have an idea," Charlie said. He crouched down at the edge of the bank and whispered something the kids couldn't hear. He then stood up again, satisfied, and wondering if his powers would do what he just attempted. Nothing happened at first, but then, slowly, the water began to bubble. It started off with only a few, but gradually more and more bubbles appeared. Suddenly a massive head appeared. It was a turtle – the size of a tractor wheel! Then three more turtles broke the surface, one after another. The four turtles swam over to the kids, allowing them to climb on top of their broad shells.

"Go! Tell your family and friends that we'll defeat Rager and they'll soon be safe to repair their town," Katie shouted across to Ethan, as the turtles swam towards the opposite bank.

"Make your way south-west from here. Keep going until you get to a wood. I'll meet you there with some of the villagers," Ethan shouted back. And with that he turned away and ran back in the direction of a ruined house.

Once they reached the opposite bank, the four children thanked the turtles and set off once more.

"I wish we had arrived there sooner," Charlie said, "because then we could have helped and stopped the zhouls from destroying the village." The others agreed with him, each wondering how they would feel if it had been their home that was destroyed.

They couldn't stop talking and thinking about their new powers, and wondering what else they could do with them. They were so engrossed in their conversation that only Daniel saw the eagle in the sky circling over them. He was about to mention it when he tripped on a tree root and immediately forgot about it. Had they noticed the eagle, they probably would have thought it strange that it appeared to be following them. It's a shame they didn't see it because this wasn't an eagle hunting for food; it had its eyes firmly on the four because it was a spy for Rager!

The friends walked all day until they reached a wood. It must have been the one Ethan was talking about, because the next wood from where they were now, according to the map Rizley had given them, was another twenty kilometres away.

The trees were magnificent. They were huge – far larger than any trees the children had ever seen before. They had leaves in all colours: greens and yellows and blues and oranges. Some of the trees had bright flowers all over them, with pollen so thick it was like a cloud blowing in the breeze. The scent was wonderful.

They set up camp just outside the wood, in case any zhouls were in there and so that they could see them coming, and also to have easy access to firewood. After eating some food from their backpack and having a drink, Charlie, Daniel and Alice tried to get some sleep, while Katie took the first watch. There were a lot of strange noises coming from the wood and Katie didn't know whether or not they were friend or foe. She was quite nervous and restless. When it was time for Alice's shift she told her about all the commotion and that it was probably nothing, but to keep an eye out just in case.

"Maybe they don't like the fire," Alice suggested, adding more logs to the dying embers and shifting them with a stick until they caught alight.

It was later on in the night, when the three moons were up, that Charlie awoke to hearing someone whispering his name. Daniel was on watch now – he was the last watch until the morning – and he looked slightly worried. He told Charlie how the noises and creatures were getting louder and how he could hear howls and angry growls getting closer.

"I said I would wake you up as I didn't want to worry the girls if it's nothing," Daniel explained. "But if it is something then one of us could hold them off while the other one wakes the girls." Charlie agreed with this plan.

They made the fire bigger yet again, but it didn't exactly stop the noises. The boys were getting nervous now and expecting a fight, when suddenly they spotted a pair of eyes staring at them …

Chapter 3

THE SPY

The eagle had circled around the children until it understood the kids' plan; where they would camp and which way they would take to get to the Tallest Mountain. That was all the information it needed. It rose into the purple sky, flew over the trees and past the floating rocks straight towards the Tallest Mountain to report what it had learned.

The Tallest Mountain was a dark, scary place. The summit was always covered in black, swirling clouds and thunder rolled constantly. There was a cave opening about halfway up the mountain, and the eagle went straight in there. He followed the tunnel deep inside and found his evil master sitting in front of a green fire. The eagle flew onto his outstretched arm and, speaking in a language that very few could understand, told him everything he had seen. Rager fed him a treat and sent him back to find out more about his unexpected visitors.

So, they are coming to me, he thought. *How helpful – that saves me the trouble of having to find to them. Now I will just prepare for their arrival.* Then he summoned the very best squad from his zhoul army and told them to set a trap for the friends when they arrived.

"Don't kill them," he warned. "I need them alive."

The squad went off to listen to the sergeant of the zhouls. "We're going to use archery," commanded the sergeant. "That way we can attack from the Archer's Point without putting ourselves into harm's way. Now we must practise and be at our best. Our master's life is in our hands. Hit the targets until you keep getting the bullseye. Then when you have mastered that, start on the moving targets and keep practising until you've mastered that too." There was a grunt of agreement throughout the squad. "Good, now go!" ordered the sergeant. *I will not let you down, Master*, he promised to himself.

Chapter 4

HELP AT LAST

T he girls woke up just as a young, strong, fit man came towards them from the woods. He had long black hair, a hard jawline and blue eyes and was of average height. He introduced himself as Robert and he was one of Ethan's neighbours. He explained to them that Ethan had said that they were here to help defeat Rager and his army, and asked if this was true. The kids told him that it was and he explained to them that there was a small group of men who wanted to help them reach the Tallest Mountain: he offered to bring the children to meet the others.

He said it was dangerous for them to stay out in the open, and that they would be safer with him. They were very glad of his help, so they followed him into the woods, through the multicoloured trees, until they eventually came to a hidden camp where there were about thirty men waiting for them, including Ethan. The kids were under the impression that Robert was in charge of the team and Ethan was second-in-command, which was interesting as he was only around the same age as them.

There was still more than an hour until morning, but the children were hungry as well as tired. The men gave them some stew that they had cooked over a camp fire. The kids thanked them for their generosity and then the team told them to get some rest.

"We have a long day ahead, so it is best if you all sleep for a few hours before we have to leave," Ethan told them.

The friends felt like they were only asleep for a few seconds when Ethan woke them again. The two suns were up, both looking like they were competing to see which would be highest and brightest; it looked like it was going to be a warm day.

Ethan and his team cleared up the camp and the whole group set off through the woods together. He told them that they must be careful, because Rager had spies everywhere.

"He probably knows that you are here already," he warned them.

"What kind of spies does he have?" asked Alice, looking fearfully all around her.

"It depends," explained Ethan. "Sometimes it is an animal that watches us from the trees or bushes. Other times it is a bird in the sky or just one of the zhouls from his army."

Daniel remembered the strange bird he had seen the day before, and he told Ethan about this. Ethan looked worried. He told Robert and they decided to send a squad of scouts, called Squad Eagle Eyes (nicknamed S.E.E.), to make sure the way was safe. He told them to report back every half hour.

Chapter 5

THE AMBUSH

When the scouts didn't report back after half an hour, Robert became worried. He spoke quietly to the other men, and Robert then sent another scout squad, this one called Squad Alpha Wolf (nicknamed S.A.W.). S.A.W. then disappeared into the woods to find their comrades.

"We need to pick up the pace," Robert explained to the children. "Something has happened to S.E.E., so we must be close to Rager's army. He must already know that you are on the way."

They hurried through the woods, and soon they met up with S.A.W. The squad leader, Jacob, said that they found some equipment belonging to S.E.E., but it was damaged with blade- and teeth-marks, and there was no sign of the scouts themselves.

They found some large animal-like footprints in the mud, which Ethan recognised from all over his village, so it was decided that they would follow them quickly, but carefully. The tracks lead them to a stone bridge over a ravine, with molten lava bubbling and steaming below.

Suddenly they spotted the zhouls on the other side of the bridge, carrying Squad Eagle Eyes. Every member was tied up, and being handled mercilessly. Without warning, one of zhouls turned his head in the direction of the men and the four friends. They were hidden in some bushes, because Robert had heard them and had told everyone to hide so they were not seen, but the kids felt like the zhoul was looking directly at them. The zhoul sniffed the air a few times and then with one enormous pound his fist came crashing down onto the stone bridge. The stone started to crack and crumble, and then with a roar it collapsed and fell into the lava deep below it.

As the children stared at dust rising out of the ravine – all that was left of the fallen bridge – they didn't hear anything behind them until it was too late. Suddenly, around a dozen zhouls leapt down out from some of the trees. It was a trap!

The men told the children to stay back, and rushed at the zhouls with their weapons, which were mostly pick-axes and pitchforks. Robert had a sword because he used to be a soldier, although the kids didn't know this yet. Some only had spades and shovels, but that didn't stop them. A big battle began, and the children tried to stay back. They watched to see how these fearsome creatures attacked. As the battle raged on, Robert shouted to the children, "Get out of here! We'll deal with these zhouls. We have fought them before – we can beat them again. Can you find a way over the ravine?"

Katie shouted back, "Yes – I can get us across. Are you sure you don't need our help here?"

"Go!" shouted Ethan. "Follow the creatures. They are headed for the Tallest Mountain. They will lead you where you need to go. Oh, and please try to rescue our friends if you can. They can help you. They know the way to the Tallest Mountain and will add to your numbers!"

"We will!" shouted all the children simultaneously, as Katie started to swing her arms around above her head. As she did so, the air seemed to move with her, faster and faster, spinning around like a tornado. "Hold on to each other," instructed Katie, and all the friends grabbed each other tightly. The tornado lifted them into the air and carried them easily across the deep ravine and set them down on the other side.

As they ran off in the direction of the creatures and their hostages, they looked back to see the battle was still fierce on the far side of the ravine. *I hope they will be ok*, thought each of the children silently, and then they disappeared into the woods once again.

Chapter 6

ZTARAS

As they went further into the woods they found more zhoul footprints, which made them a bit more scared. Even though they had awesome powers, they saw the damage these creatures could do. Eventually the giant footprints split up, going in several different directions.

"Great. How are we going to find the scouts now?" asked Alice in frustration. "And I have a bad feeling about this place. It's perfect for another ambush."

"I have an idea," said Katie. "If I can fly high enough I will hopefully be able to see the zhouls."

"No, don't; if you do you'll have to fly higher than the trees and then they'll know exactly where we are. Even if you do find them, what will we do then?" asked Alice, reluctant to cross paths with the zhouls once again.

"Well, it's worth a try, isn't it?" asked Daniel, with a reassuring grin. "And we'll decide what to do when we find them ... if we get to that point."

Alice sighed. "Knock yourself out," she said to Katie.

So Katie concentrated and connected with the air and started to ascend. When she was above the trees she stopped and looked around a few times. "I don't see any sign of them," she called.

"Ok, good job. Come on back down," replied Daniel. "There, you see Alice? Nothing to worry about."

As Katie descended, she thought she saw something move. There it was again. Her eyes widened with a frightening realisation.

"Guys! Look out!" she shouted and picked up speed, but it was too late. Zhouls jumped out of some bushes. Two grabbed each kid and pinned them to the ground by the arms. Six archers surrounded Katie and aimed their weapons at her. One of the zhouls stood out more than the others. He had two more zhouls following behind him like bodyguards. He looked up at Katie.

"There's no escape. Come down and no one will get hurt." His voice boomed up at her. Katie's jaw dropped.

"How ...?" Alice began, but the zhoul interrupted her. "My name is Ztaras and I am the only zhoul who can speak the human language."

Reluctantly, Katie came down and was also immediately grabbed by the arms by two more zhouls.

Then Charlie spotted the team of captured scouts who were being led out of the bushes. They were all tied up and being pushed along mercilessly. The sight made his blood boil.

"What do you want with them?" he asked, nodding in their direction, fighting hard not to let his anger show. The zhouls roared with laughter and Ztaras said, "We attacked and kidnapped them because we knew you would come and try to rescue them."

Daniel, however, wasn't really listening. He realised that he could feel his friend's anger and channel this hot and angry feeling. He whispered "Fire!" and then fire flew out of his hands and straight at the two zhouls holding his arms. The zhouls roared in pain as the fire spread over them. Then he shouted "Fire!" again and more came out of his hands straight towards the zhouls holding the scouts hostage. The zhouls tried to dodge the fire, but they couldn't. As the fire reached them, it burned the ropes off the scouts who then ran as fast as they could to the children. Katie, Alice, and Charlie broke free of the zhouls' grasp and each used their power to push their captors away and give themselves some breathing space. Just then, Robert, Ethan and the rest of his team came running out of some nearby bushes.

"Back so soon?" asked Charlie, smiling.

"Why, did you miss us?" Ethan asked, smiling back.

"We just about beat the zhouls who had ambushed us and spent the rest of our time trying to figure out how to get across the ravine," Robert said from behind Ethan.

"Were they a bit of trouble? Could you have done with our help after all?" Daniel smirked.

"Hey!" Robert said. "We managed and are here now, so no, we were fine.'
"Thanks!" interrupted one of the rescued scouts.

"Don't thank us yet," Daniel replied. "That fire is spreading fast and coming this way."

"Come on – let's get out of here," Alice added.

The fire spread to the closest bushes and trees and quickly surrounded both groups splitting the zhouls from the others.

"Be careful which way you go," warned Daniel. "The fire is too hot – do you want to be scorched?"

Alice looked like she was about to object but Charlie interrupted him.

"I can clear an escape route for us," he said. "And if I judge the amount of water right, then the fire should spread over it again."

"Eh, guys, I hate to interrupt, but we are really running out of time, fast! The zhouls are starting to recover already, and are looking for a way around the fire!" interrupted Katie.

And so Charlie sprayed water to clear a path and they ran off towards the Tallest Mountain, with the entire team together once again.

Chapter 7

THE MOUNTAIN

As they approached the mountain, the children realised they didn't have a plan to access it. Alice said that she had an idea for her power and wanted to try it out. So it was agreed that they would let Alice get them access. They all stepped out over the border between the woods and the clearing, which surrounded the Tallest Mountain. It was so high that when the children tried to see the summit it looked as if it curved over them. It made them quite dizzy. The top was surrounded by dark, swirling clouds, which were lit up by frequent bolts of lightning. It was also hard to hear anything around the mountain because of the constant thunder.

Alice put her hands on the ground and concentrated as hard as she could, ignoring the hundreds of zhouls that had emerged from the mountain and were running towards the group. Suddenly two giant hands made of rock and earth formed and rose up from the ground. Then Alice lifted her hands off the ground and started to open and close them. The earth hands opened and closed as well, but the only difference was that the earth hands were grabbing up zhoul guards and chucking them overhead, like a kid throwing a doll over his shoulder.

The children couldn't help laughing as the zhouls went flying through the air, deep into the woods behind. But more and more guards kept coming out of the mountain, and even the earth hands couldn't cope with them all. Just then an aircraft flew out of a hangar in the side of the mountain and started shooting green balls of acid towards them.

"We're all going to have to lend a hand to the hands!" shouted Robert over the thunder. "Come on!"

Everyone laughed as they ran towards the zhouls. Alice's earth hands kept bashing more and more guards, but now the other three started using their powers too, along with Robert's and Ethan's team fighting for their defence. The kids would each take out some zhouls at the front and the team would move into the zhouls' old places so they could move forward and hold their position. This way they had a steady perimeter advancing on the mountain and protecting the kids. Charlie seemed to be able to suck water out of the ground and air around him and was firing water jets at the zhouls. Daniel was shooting fire at the aircraft and blowing up the acid balls as they shot towards them. One acid ball landed on a rock close by, and they watched it dissolve the rock into nothing in seconds.

Alice fumed. "I was going to throw that rock at the aircraft," she said, clearly annoyed.

"We have to take out the aircraft if we want to get to the mountain!" shouted Robert.

I know what to do, thought Alice. She put her hands on the ground and concentrated hard once again. *If I can't catapult a rock I'm just going to have to use something else.* A cone emerged from the ground, followed by a long cylinder, followed by three thin triangles, all made of rock. Alice closed her eyes for the next part because she really had to concentrate. The rock objects suddenly shot together as if they were magnetic, then stuck to each other, forming one whole object.

"A missile," gasped Charlie. "Of course!" One earth hand lifted it up, the point facing the aircraft. The other hand flicked it up towards the aircraft and it went flying through it with a crash, coming out the other side! Then the aircraft started to sway to the right as it came falling to the ground.

"Take cover!" shouted Daniel. The children and the others dived behind some huge boulders but the zhouls weren't as lucky.

The crash and explosion from the aircraft was deafening; by comparison, it made the thunder sound like a whisper. When their ears stopped ringing and the dust cleared, only then did they emerge from their hiding spot. There was debris everywhere, and a large hole where acid had burned into the ground.

"I did it!" said Alice in surprise.

"We better move quickly, before more guards come," suggested Robert. Suddenly they heard a whistling noise. They looked up and saw Alice's missile coming back. Alice pointed to an area on the mountain. The missile responded and flew into it making both the face of the mountain at that point, and the missile, crumble to dust, revealing a big wooden door.

"Just plaster," remarked Alice. "With a hidden door."

"How did you ...?" asked Katie.

Alice shrugged. "Just a hunch. Plus there were more guards in that area than anywhere else. And somehow I could sense that it wasn't rock."

"Can I do the honours?" pleaded Katie.

"Sure," replied Alice.

"Yes!" Katie said as she blew the door right off its hinges (good thing they weren't going for stealth) revealing a well-lit opening with some wooden stairs going up around the far side. The stairs led to a stone balcony, which had an arched open stone doorway at the end.

"Rager, here we come," murmured Daniel.

"We're in," said Charlie loudly. Suddenly a giant bat-like creature glided down from the roof. It stopped about two metres off the ground and hovered there, in the middle of the room. It roared and bared its teeth at them.

"Me and my big mouth," muttered Charlie.

Chapter 8

THE DRABONZ

" A drabonz ..." Robert's voice trailed off as the beast roared again.

"Run!" shouted Alice. Everyone ran around the inside of the mountain with the creature slashing its tail and claws and snapping its jaws at them whilst flapping its wings to keep hovering. Some of Robert's team tried to go up the stairs to the next level of the mountain, but the drabonz bit the wooden poles that were holding the stairs up and they collapsed. Others tried to hide, but it didn't help much. Katie was getting annoyed with the drabonz because it was roaring so often. After another roar Katie shouted "Arghhh! Shut up!" The bat-like creature seemed stunned for a second. It paused and turned face to her, but then it just roared back in her face.

Katie took a deep breath. "That's it!" she said in anger. She concentrated and 'connected' with one of the wooden poles from the stairs and used the pole to bash the drabonz on the head, right out of the air. When it tried to fly away she just knocked it back down. When it stopped fighting Katie stopped too. She was panting as she blew the pole back to the splintered remains of the stairs.

As soon as the pole landed with a loud snap the bat got up dizzily, red-eyed with anger.

Everyone was too frightened to scream or shout. Once it regained its balance, its mouth began to glow white. Suddenly it started shooting bolts of electricity at the team and the friends. After each bolt its head recoiled. One of the men from the team was so scared he walked backwards and tripped over the giant creature's tail. It turned to face him and fired more of the bolts at him. He ran screaming and shouting out the way they had come in. The bat followed, shooting more and more balls at him, but once it was in the sunlight and tried to fire, it electrocuted itself. It could only work in the dark! It tried to get out of the light, but the kids stopped it.

"Oh, no you don't," Katie declared as she blew it back into the sunlight. That made the bat so mad it tried to fire and electrocuted itself again.

"Poor thing, did you forget your weakness?" Alice teased as she made another missile and threw it at the bat.

The creature flew up into the air to try to outrun Alice's attack, but the missile just followed. The bat was still weak after electrocuting itself so it couldn't fly as fast as before. The missile picked up speed and then BANG! It struck a hole in the bat's wing and crumbled to dust. The bat roared in pain and started to fall. The children watched as it disappeared into the ravine. Suddenly they heard a loud sizzling noise.

"Bats are nocturnal, right?" said Alice. "Remember, for homework back at school, we had to read a page in one of our books and it was about bats? I think we interrupted its sleep."

"Could also have something to do with its weakness, now that I think about it," said Robert.

"That wasn't too bad now, was it? It was kinda fun," Katie said.

"Don't get too cocky – we've got a long way to go yet," added Daniel.

"Relax, we just took out nearly half of Rager's army and one of his airships," said Charlie, grinning like a maniac.

"Come on, let's finish our job!" said Ethan.

"Yeah, let's go" Charlie declared.

The kids and Robert's team ran back to the mountain, full of confidence.

Chapter 9

THE PLAN

D eep inside the mountain, Ztaras, the zhoul sergeant, told Rager that the children had defeated the drabonz.

"They are more powerful than I thought, but that is good," he said, once Ztaras had explained the situation. "It's time for me to put my plan to steal their powers into action. But use the defences so there is no suspicion."

"Yes sir," came the reply. "Send in squad numbers three and four to attack," he spoke in the zhouls' language, Zhouldish. "And prepare to activate Operation Steal and Absorb."

*

When the children got back and remembered that the stairs were broken they had to think of another way to climb up. But it didn't take long because Katie created a wind that carried them all safely to the top. At the summit, Charlie asked Alice to make a ramp in case they needed to get out fast. Just as she was about to start, they heard an ear-splitting roar and saw zhouls running out of the arched stone doorway and heading straight for them on the other side of the balcony.

Alice heard their battle cries and a look of worry crossed her face.

"Keep going, we'll deal with these guys," said Katie, encouraging her to continue with her task. Alice concentrated. Just as she finished making the ramp, the battle fell down to where they fought the drabonz.

Daniel was shooting fire balls at the zhouls and they were running around, trying desperately to put out the fire. Katie was pushing and pulling the zhouls against the walls and Daniel's zhouls kept getting hit by hers. Charlie was forcing them back with a continuous jet of water. They were trying to push through the jet but kept losing their balance. Alice made a hole in the ground and as the zhouls toppled they were washed into it. She just stood there grinning as zhouls disappeared from view. Soon all the zhouls were gone and the children could carry on with the job. Robert told some of his team to stay and keep watch.

*

After Ztaras heard that squads three and four had been defeated, he initiated Operation Steal and Absorb. He sent his trained archers to the Archer's Point in the Walled Hall. He told Rager that he had the operation set for their arrival. Rager complimented him.

"You did well today, sergeant. I think I'll promote you to the commander of my army."

"Thank you, master," Ztaras replied.

Rager dismissed him with a wave of his hand. Ztaras left for the Archer's Point and the rest of battalion, while Rager went to prepare for his meeting with the four kids.

At last, he thought to himself, *I shall have the strongest powers in the world – no, in two worlds.* "Bring me my battle armour and my staff!" he ordered.

He was ready for the ambush.

Chapter 10

RAGER

The children and the team emerged into a big square room. Directly ahead was a large wooden door, almost exactly the same as the one they had entered through. It had four walls on the perimeter and each of those walls had a door on it. On the roof were open windows with no glass in a circle going around the room. This was called the Archer's Point. The kids and the team walked on, wondering what the room was called. They couldn't have known that it was Rager's favourite room, where he planned to defeat them. It was the Walled Hall.

The doors in front of them suddenly flew open and there was Rager himself, grinning from ear to ear. He had bright green eyes, pointed ears, purple skin, a red cape blowing behind him and blue armour shining in the light. In his hand was a long staff with a strange crystal on top that looked like it was made from a glowing red diamond.

"Well, well. We meet at last," he sneered. "Surrender or the archers will fire, with no hesitation!" He nodded to the roof. The kids and the team looked up at the Archer's Point where every window had been filled by a menacing zhoul archer.

"Make us, you rainbow-coloured freak!" shouted Alice, looking determined.

"Kids, we can handle the archers. You go after Rager, ok?" Ethan whispered. The kids nodded and Katie replied, "With pleasure."

"Good luck guys," said Robert. "Kick Rager's multi-coloured butt."

"Fire!" shouted Rager, realising their plan.

Arrows were suddenly raining down on to them. Robert and his team used shields to block the first wave of arrows, and then started to fire their own arrows at the archers. The shields were once again mostly homemade, but they did the job. As that battle took place the archers' attention was drawn away from the children, so they were left face to face Rager.

"You're no match for me, kiddies," he said, sneering at them. "What if you end up dying, fighting me? Think about how your family and friends will feel, to never know what happened to you, where you are, nor will they be able to bury the bodies. Do you really want to put them through that? Give me your powers and all that can be prevented."

Chapter 11

THE FIGHT!

T he kids stopped and looked at each other. He had a point.

"That's not going to happen!" shouted Ethan from within the battle. The kids turned to see Ethan and Robert staring at them from underneath the protection of their shields. They both nodded reassuringly.

"Hit him hard," Robert called over the sounds of the battle. "You can do this." That confirmed the kids' decision and they once again launched back into action.

"Don't need to tell me twice!" said Alice with a missile to her left and one earth hand on her right. As she threw the missile with her earth hand at Rager, she said loudly, "Is it a bird? Is it a plane? No, it's my missile!"

Rager just stood there as if the missile heading right at him at amazing speed was merely a tiny fly. When it was about two metres away from him, he pointed his staff in front of him. When the diamond touched the missile there was a big flash of light and nobody could see anything, but when the light cleared and they were able to see again, the missile was gone. And Rager was still standing there, as smug as ever.

Alice was speechless. "He ... but... how?" she stammered.

Rager said, an evil smile on his face, "Nice, huh? It's a Revelis Diamond. Very rare and very powerful. I got it from a mine that was, ahem, given to me."

"You mean you took it," said Charlie sternly.

"Well, yeah, but it's *mine* now!" He laughed at his own joke. The kids shook their heads disapprovingly. Rager stopped laughing. "What, really? Come on, that was good!"

"Enough talk, let's fight!" said Katie, rather bossily.

"You always wanted to say that, didn't you?" asked Alice, who had found her voice again.

"What, too scared to fight me, kids?" mocked Rager in a baby voice.

"Do us all a favour and shut up. Defend this!" Charlie shouted. He put his hands on the ground and thought, *It's time to go for a little swim, Rager.* Suddenly water rose out of the ground at the opposite end of the walled hall, forming a large wave. He didn't make it too big though because he didn't want the whole mountain falling down from the inside. It made its way towards Rager, gathering more and more speed and size. Again, Rager just stood there. Like before, as it went over him there was a big flash of light but when they could see again, the water was still there.

"Ha!" Charlie shouted. Then his voiced changed as he pretended to be respectful and sad. "And here we have the resting place of the not-at-all-admirable Rager. He won't be missed." Charlie began laughing hysterically.

But when the water cleared they saw Rager: he was in a red force field and the crystal on his staff was pulsing.

"Oh," was all Charlie could manage.

"Was that meant for me?" Rager mocked.

"It's my turn!" shouted Katie in anger. "Hope you like my latest power tactic. Alice throw up a boulder, please!" she commanded. While the boulder was in the air Katie started spinning faster and faster. As she spun a tornado appeared and the boulder fell into it. Katie suddenly stopped spinning and pushed her hands towards Rager and the boulder flew through the air at him. He just stood there again. When it was within range, he tipped the boulder and cracks appeared with white light coming out of them. Suddenly there was a huge KA–BOOM! and the boulder exploded. A piece flew towards Rager and he just stepped to the side.

Without warning Daniel started moving his hands slowly over each other as if there were an invisible glass ball between them. A small spark came into view when he moved them faster. Faster and faster went his hands; bigger and bigger went the fireball. Suddenly he thrust his hands towards Rager (who was still mocking Katie) and the fireball flew at him.

Rager had to dive to the side when the fireball came at him. The ball turned around and flew towards him again. This time Rager was paying attention and dodged to the side, then jabbed his staff into it but even the kids could see through the white light that he was sweating. Maybe they were getting to him after all.

Chapter 12

AT LAST!

S uddenly a plan formed in Daniel's head
while Rager was shouting at them. "Oh, you
think you're so smart! Well, I'll have you
know I captured your attacks inside my Revelis
Diamond, yeah, that's what a Revelis Diamond
does, captures whatever attacks it! Now I'm able
to use those captured attacks against you! HA!"
But the kids weren't listening, because Daniel
was already telling his plan to the others. "We
need to surround him and attack at different
sides," he was telling the others. "That way he
won't know which one of us will attack next."

So they worked their way into different parts
of the room until they had surrounded him. At
first, everything went as planned. Rager stood in
the middle facing each one of them in turn, until
Katie tried to create a tornado and it all went

wrong. She was blasted back and hit the wall behind her. Daniel, Alice and Charlie, shocked by what had happened, ran over to her to see if she was alright. While they were looking at her she just said in a quiet voice, "Behind you ..." The three of them spun around just in time to see a red light flash out of Rager's staff, and then one of Katie's tornadoes shooting one of Alice's missiles headed straight for them! They dived aside and it crashed into the wall above Katie, showering her with debris and dust.

"I don't know how you did that to Katie, but you won't get away with that again!" Daniel called.

"Oh, yes I will" said Rager calmly.

"How did you do that?" called Alice. "Tell us!"

"I already did," replied Rager, grinning.

"Liar!" shouted Charlie. He was very angry.

"Now, now. That's no way to talk to me is it now children? And I really did, but all of you were too busy talking to listen to Uncle Rager," he exclaimed sarcastically.

"Oh, when I was explaining my idea!" said Daniel angrily blaming himself for not listening and distracting the others. He just hoped that the plan would work now.

"So that's what you were doing" mocked Rager. "Well, I guess you should have been paying more attention."

The three of them were so angry and frustrated they all carried out their strongest, or rather, favoured, attack: Alice did her missile, Charlie did his wave and Daniel did his fireball. But, just like Katie's, those attacks were also trapped in the Revelis Diamond, and they were blasted back into the wall.

Mix your powers, said a voice. The kids looked around, frantically trying to find out where the voice was coming from, then at each other to see if anyone else had heard it too. They all wore the same confused expression. Someone was talking to them from inside their heads. The voice was familiar, but they couldn't quite place it.

Combine all the powers, the voice sounded urgent. *When the four powers are together they create a fifth power that cannot be beaten.*

Alice, who was nearest to Daniel, said, "That's how we can beat him." The other three nodded and looked over at Rager.

"I'm sorry to interrupt your chat, but there is a battle going on, in case you haven't noticed," said Rager in his usual mocking voice.

"Yeah, we've noticed!" said Katie. "And we've just figured out how to beat you!" Then she muttered, "We think," under her breath. Rager's face turned from a mocking smile to an annoying smirk.

"Beat me? You think you can beat me? Impossible! You kids will never be able to defeat me. Never!" laughed Rager, with a really ugly, evil smile.

It's time, said the voice in their heads. *Now!*

The kids reacted as one. "Fire, water, wind, earth!" all four cried.

In a flash of white light they each held a tennis-ball-sized white orb. Each orb seemed to contain all of their powers combined into one.

You throw it. It hits him. He is defeated. We celebrate. We all live happily ever after, said the voice. It made it sound so easy.

Rager stood there in awe. *It wasn't meant to work,* he thought. *I took their most powerful powers. I didn't think the fifth power actually existed.*

Now the voice was explaining to the kids what they needed to do.

You only have one shot at this each. If one of you misses, all of you fail, understand? They nodded. *Good. Now go and beat him. I know you won't fail me.*

"We need a plan," said Katie, but Daniel already knew what to do.

"We use the same tactic as earlier. That's the best and easiest way to get him. When his back is turned to one of us, throw your ball, but don't make it too obvious. Take your time and, well ... don't miss." They nodded. "Good, now let's beat this guy!" he cried.

As they surrounded Rager for the second time and he saw they were each in a throwing position, he figured out what they were up to. Soon he was turning from one kid to another, trying to keep them all in his view at once.

It was Alice who threw her ball first when Rager was facing Charlie. Rager heard her and spun around, swinging his staff to try and capture it, but missed. It hit him in the chest and he fell over, but got back up just as fast. *The orbs make me weaker,* he realised as his armour cracked and fell off.

He turned to attack Alice and then Charlie threw his ball. Rager heard him throw and spun; this time his staff smacked into the orb. However, it was in vain. His staff was thrown through the air and away from him, Rager just managing to keep hold of the precious Revelis Diamond. He turned around, facing Daniel, and Katie threw her ball at him. This time the diamond cracked and crumbled to dust and Rager cried out. He half turned in anger to shout at Katie and instantly knew he had made his final mistake. But it was too late and, last but not least, Daniel threw his ball at him and he fell onto all fours.

"You ... kids ... can't ... defeat ... me!" he managed to wheeze.

"Eh, we already did! Now whose friends and family are gonna be looking for them! It's time for some solitary confinement!" cried Alice happily.

"We did it, we actually did it!" said Charlie in disbelief.

"Oh yeah, in your face Rager!" cried Katie, and wiggled a victory dance.

"No way did we just do what I think we did. We saved Willōga, we saved Willōga!" Daniel chanted, punching the air in happiness.

But Ztaras, the leader of the archers, overheard Daniel's chanting and saw his master on his hands and knees.

"Retreat!" he shouted in Zhouldish. "General's down! Retreat!" The zhouls stopped firing the arrows and took off, with Ztaras in the lead.

"Get back here you cowards!" shouted Robert, but stopped after he heard Daniel chanting. "They did it!" he muttered happily and then shouted to his team. "The four kids saved Willōga!" They knew straight away what he meant and there was a roar of cheers. "The four kids!" was shouted and cheered over and over again.

Robert and Ethan ran up to the children.

"Hey you guys, you did it! Well done! Oh boy, we've got to tell the queen about this!" The kids stopped in their tracks.

"The queen?" asked Charlie, nervously. "Are you sure that's a good idea?"

"I think it's a great idea!" said Alice, happily.

"Fine by me!" said Daniel.

"Sounds cool!" said Katie.
"Then it's settled, we're going to the queen!" replied Robert.

"You know," Robert began proudly, after they were out of the mountain and on their way to the castle, "I used to be one of her bodyguards."

"Really?" asked Charlie. "What was it like?"

"Oh man, it was awesome," said Robert with a sigh. And then almost as an afterthought,

"John, Jack – drag him along with us." He nodded to Rager, who was trying to crawl away.

Three hours later, they emerged at the huge castle doors. Two guards were standing on top of the enormous wall that surrounded the castle. The guard on the right called down, "Who are you and what's your business here?"

Robert replied for everyone, his voice suddenly professional and business-like, and exclaimed, "Commander Robert reporting. I am here with the four saviours. We have the evil lord, Rager, in our custody."

The guard's eyes widened. "You defeated Rager? I mean ..." He coughed. "You have defeated the evil lord?"

"Affirmative."

"Display evidence of what you claim."

The four kids stepped out of the crowd and lined up in a row. Daniel made a fire ball in his hand, Charlie made a water ball in his hand, Katie made a tornado in her hand and Alice made earth rise in front of her feet. John and Jack also stepped forward, dragging Rager between them. Rager's head was down, staring at the ground.

The guards looked at them and then the guard on the right said, "You have verified yourselves. You may go in. Sorry about that, Robert, but you know how the queen is about her security, especially seeing as we needed to protect her from Rager."

Robert replied, "It's ok, Wayne, I understand you must conduct security checks as are your orders. And how are you, Tom?" He nodded to the other guard.

"Fine, fine, thanks for asking," Tom replied. "Oh my goodness, it's over. Finally, my kids can play safely outside again. Well, in you go then. Hey George, open the gate!" Tom shouted at someone behind the walls.

The gate started to rise up slowly. When it was fully opened, a patrol of soldiers, two cavalry and four swordsmen, came out and took Rager away by the arms.

When they had disappeared, Tom turned to Robert and the kids and said, "In you go then, see you Robert!"

"Yeah, I'll see you, Tom." replied Robert. Then he turned to the guard on the left. "Bye, Wayne."

"Nice talking to you, Robert," said Wayne in reply.

Chapter 13

THE QUEEN

The castle was amazing. The courtyards were full of stables, horse-racing tracks and soldiers training down in the barracks. The castle building itself was made of stone, as were the walls, and it looked like master craftsmen had built it all. And the pictures inside the castle were so well painted it was like they were real people. But the hall, the huge rectangular Great Hall, was the best of all! There was a big long table running in the middle of the room. There were torches between each half oval window. And at the back of the table was a big golden throne where the queen herself sat with two fully armoured bodyguards standing at her side.

"Your majesty!" announced Robert, bowing deeply with respect.

"Ah, Commander Robert! What brings you to the castle?" asked the queen, kindly.

"Well, your majesty, these four kids ..." said Robert gently pushing the friends forward,"... have defeated the evil lord, Rager." The queen's eyes widened.

From behind the queen's throne a young girl appeared. She was around the same age as the four friends and had black hair and when she spoke she sounded as sweet and kind as the queen. Her name was Princess Maeve.

"Mum?" she said. "Can I go for a few rides round the horse track with Speedy?" Speedy was Princess Maeve's horse. He was called Speedy because none of the other horses in the castle (and the horses in the castle were the fastest in the land) had beaten him in speed, strength or skill, despite it not being a very original name.

"Ah, Maeve you're just in time! These four wonderful children have beaten the dark lord, Rager. Am I right to think that you are quite tired?" the queen asked, kindly.

Suddenly the four friends realised they were in fact very tired. They hadn't rested since they first met Robert and the team.

They looked hesitantly back at Robert and Ethan. The two of them nodded. "Yes, your majesty!" the four said simultaneously.

"I thought as much. Maeve, please show our guests to their rooms. The best rooms," said the queen.

"Yes, mother," replied Maeve.

She looked at the kids and beckoned them to follow her. The four friends followed her up some stairs to two great bedrooms with separate beds in each one. "This is the boys' room," said Maeve, showing the boys their room. It had two enormous beds with a half-oval window, similar to the ones in the Great Hall, in between. The boys chose a bed each before coming out again to see the girls' room.

"And this is the girls' room" said Maeve. It was more or less the same as the boys' room.

"Now, only have a quick nap. If I know my mum then she'll definitely do something to celebrate. What, though, I don't know. Probably have a feast. Again." Maeve sounded bored at the idea. " I'll come and get you in a while. Now I'm going off to the race track. See you later!" And with a wave of her hand she skipped off down the stairs.

When the boys woke up Maeve was standing in their room, wearing a beautiful dress.

"Wakey, wakey rise 'n' shine sleepy heads!" said Maeve happily. "The girls are already at the celebration! Come on! Oh and by the way, your clothes have been washed and dried and are ready for you."

The boys tumbled out of bed and changed out of the pyjamas they had been supplied with. Maeve waited outside, and when the boys had finished they followed her downstairs.

As they entered the Great Hall they saw a massive feast on the long table. The Great Hall immediately fell silent.

"As you all very well know we are holding this feast in honour of the four saviours!" announced the queen.

There was a cheer throughout the huge chamber.

"Thanks to them, Willōga is safe once again. If it wasn't for them, my kingdom and the world would still be living in fear. So therefore, hip hip!" The entire room launched into a tremendous "Hooray!"

"Hip hip!"

"Hooray!"

"Hip hip!"

"Hooray!"

"Now," the queen announced, "let the feast begin!"

There was everything! From the meat (which was cooked to perfection) to the vegetables (which were the sweetest and most delicious). And the dessert – well the desert was like there was a party in your mouth!

When they couldn't eat another bite a young man came over. "Excuse me, but are you the four saviours?" he asked.

"I suppose so, yes. Why?" Alice spoke for the others.

"Follow me please," said the man.

He led them out of the castle and through the gates and when they turned a corner a quaint little cottage appeared into view. The sight seemed oddly familiar. There was smoke coming from the chimney and when the man knocked on the door it creaked open of its own accord. They walked into a small, peculiar, yet once again familiar, room and their escort left them and closed the door behind him.

"Welcome back!" said a familiar voice.

The children turned swiftly around and there sitting on a chair was Rizley, the man who had helped them at the start of their adventure. Suddenly the kids knew where they were.

"Why don't you have a seat," he invited kindly, as four chairs gently nudged the children from behind.

"Have a seat and I'll explain everything!" The kids sat down. "First, let me introduce myself properly. I am Rizley, the castle wizard."

"You're a wizard? Is that how we arrived in Willōga? Was it your voice in our heads?" asked Charlie, both amazed and confused.

"Yes and yes. I did both those things, along with the things you already know about," replied Rizley, with a sense of delight at his own cleverness.

"But how did you know that mixing our powers would work?" Alice asked.

Rizley shrugged. "I've seen visions, made a couple of potions as tests, tried an example of it myself, so I was pretty confident".

"If you're a wizard, where's your hat, robe and wand?" asked Katie wonderingly.

"My wand is here," Rizley said, taking his wand out of his sleeve. "My hat is on the coat hanger behind the door and my robe is in my wardrobe upstairs but don't believe everything you read in books. I got them as a present from a friend who has quite a sense of humour. Well, except the wand. Obviously."

"Did you call us here to bring us back home?" asked Daniel thoughtfully.

"Well, yes, but I wanted to talk to you as well," replied Rizley. "You see, I believe we will need you, and your magnificent powers, again in the future. Would you mind terribly, should an occasion arise, if I summon you here? I must admit, it might not be very glamorous, but needs must! And also, would you mind if I summoned you at any time?"

He waited for them to say something but they were lost for words so he took advantage of their silence.

"I believe this may be the start of something big. Think about it very carefully before I send you home." And with that he went off into the kitchen, humming merrily to himself.

The kids whispered to each other in low voices. Eventually, they came to an agreement and went to look for Rizley. When they opened the kitchen door they saw him sitting at the table talking to a young girl who was about their age.

"Ah, I see you have made your minds up. But first let me introduce my daughter, Rebecca,"

Rizley said, nodding towards the young girl. Rebecca waved and said "hi" cheerily. She had a friendly smile and the kids immediately knew they would get along.

"So you've made up your mind?" asked Rizley.

"Yes," said Katie. "We'd like to help in any way we can, and no, we won't mind if there isn't much warning. But, just wondering, does time still move in our world while we're here?"

"Well, the thing about that is that, no, it doesn't continue while you're here … so don't be concerned about your families missing you, or anything like that." He sounded proud.

"Oh great, I was worried I'd have to explain all this to my parents!" Katie laughed.

"Ok then, ready to go home?" Rizley asked.

The kids nodded.

"Thanks for saving Willōga. Until next time!"

"Bye," said Rebecca, as she waved goodbye.

Rizley cracked his knuckles, muttered something under his breath and waved his wand. The kids felt themselves starting to fade away. They closed their eyes and when they opened them again they were back in their world, right in front of their classroom door, exactly where they had been when they left.

They didn't have much time to think about their adventure, since their teacher had decided the class needed to prepare for their end-of-year test.

"Next time, tell Rizley to drop us back *after* the tests," Alice said as they walked home after school. They all laughed in agreement.

This was the beginning of their many adventures. As Rizley said, it was the start of something big!

19205076R00048

Printed in Great Britain
by Amazon